The Mystery of the Book Fair

THREE COUSINS DETECTIVE CLUB®

99C

The Mystery of the Book Fair

Elspeth Campbell Murphy

Illustrated by Joe Nordstrom

BETHANY HOUSE PUBLISHERS
MINNEAPOLIS, MINNESOTA 55438

The Mystery of the Book Fair
Copyright © 1999
Elspeth Campbell Murphy

Cover and story illustrations by Joe Nordstrom

Scripture quotations are from the *International Children's Bible, New Century Version,* copyright © 1986, 1988 by Word Publishing, Dallas, Texas 75039. Used by permission.

Published by Bethany House Publishers
A Ministry of Bethany Fellowship International
11400 Hampshire Avenue South
Minneapolis, Minnesota 55438
www.bethanyhouse.com

Printed in the United States of America by
Bethany Press International, Minneapolis, Minnesota 55438

Library of Congress Cataloging-in-Publication Data

Murphy, Elspeth Campbell.
    The mystery of the book fair / by Elspeth Campbell Murphy ; illustrated by Joe Nordstrom.
       p. cm. — (Three Cousins Detective Club ; 24)
    SUMMARY: When Sarah-Jane discovers that several other people want the same old favorite books which she has just found at a benefit for the library, she and her cousins find out why.
    ISBN 0–7642–2132–9
    [1. Fairs Fiction. 2. Cousins Fiction. 3. Mystery and detective stories.] I. Nordstrom, Joe, Ill. II. Title. III. Series: Murphy, Elspeth Campbell. Three Cousins Detective Club ; 24.
PZ7.M95316 Mk 1999
[Fic]—dc21   99–6449
                                              CIP

ELSPETH CAMPBELL MURPHY has been a familiar name in Christian publishing for nearly twenty years, with more than one hundred books to her credit and sales approaching six million worldwide. She is the author of the bestselling series *David and I Talk to God* and *The Kids From Apple Street Church*, as well as the 1990 Gold Medallion winner *Do You See Me, God?*, and two books of prayer meditations for teachers, *Chalkdust* and *Recess*. A graduate of Trinity College and Moody Bible Institute, Elspeth and her husband, Mike, make their home in Chicago, where she writes full time.

Contents

"Don't ever stop being kind and truthful. Let kindness and truth show in all you do. Write them down in your mind as if on a tablet."
Proverbs 3:3

1

An Excellent Reader

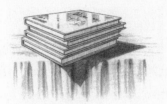

Sarah-Jane Cooper was an excellent reader.

So were her cousins Timothy Dawson and Titus McKay.

Sarah-Jane was also an excellent shopper.

That's where she and the boys parted company.

Still, Sarah-Jane had been able to get Timothy and Titus up first thing on a Saturday morning (the boys were visiting for the weekend) and haul them down to the Fairfield library for the book fair.

She had a good reason for wanting to be first in line.

And she had made it.

They were first.

That is to say, Sarah-Jane was.

Titus wasn't exactly in line. He was never at his best first thing in the morning. Right now he was slumped up against a nearby tree with his eyes closed.

Timothy wasn't in line, either. He always woke up bright and early, full of energy. Right now he was trying to peek in the windows of the multipurpose room, where the book fair was being held.

Sarah-Jane hadn't gone with him to peek in the windows. She hadn't wanted to lose their place in line.

Right behind her there were a few grown-ups. She didn't recognize any of them. They didn't speak to her or to one another. Instead, they kept tapping their feet and glancing at their watches.

She had been excited about the book fair for a long time. But now she was more than excited. The impatience of the grown-ups behind her was making her nervous.

"Did you see anything?" Sarah-Jane asked Timothy when he wandered back from the windows.

"Not really," Timothy replied. "Just lots of long tables filled with books."

Sarah-Jane nodded. That's exactly what she had expected, after all.

The Fairfield County Library, one of Sarah-Jane's favorite places in the whole world, needed to raise some money for new books and equipment. So they had asked everybody to donate used books in good condition. Those books would then go on sale at a book fair.

A dollar for hard-covers.

Fifty cents for paperbacks.

Such a deal!

Lots and lots and lots of books had come in. More than anyone had expected. Volunteers had even gone door to door collecting books. Sarah-Jane had been a part of that. So it looked as if the book fair was going to be a great success, and she was more than ready.

Normally Sarah-Jane, super shopper, had a foolproof method. She would quickly go through the whole place to get an overview. Then she would settle down and go through everything s-l-o-w-l-y.

But not today.

Today was different.

She had five dollars to spend.

It cost a dollar to get in. That left four dollars for books. And Sarah-Jane already knew *exactly* what she was going to buy.

Were they ever going to open the doors?

2

Four Little Books

No sooner had Sarah-Jane thought, *Are they ever going to open the doors?*—than the doors opened.

The impatient grown-ups and Sarah-Jane rushed inside.

She figured it was OK not to wait for her cousins. You didn't have to stick together just to browse through books, did you? Besides, Timothy had wandered off again, and Titus was still slumped against his tree. She figured they would catch up with her when they were ready.

Sarah-Jane paid her dollar at the door and got her hand stamped *Paid*. That way, if she had to leave, she could get back in without having to pay again.

Sarah-Jane made a beeline for the kids' section.

She could have gotten eight paperbacks with her four dollars. But that's not what she was after.

Whew! There they were!

Just as she hoped—knew—they would be.

Four little hard-covers in cream-colored jackets.

Sure, they were old. But they were in excellent condition. Sarah-Jane loved old things. She loved imagining where they had come from and whom they had belonged to. And most of all, Sarah-Jane suddenly realized, she loved old books.

Sarah-Jane snatched up the books and hugged them close.

One of the books was titled *Winnie-the-Pooh*. Another was called *House at Pooh Corner*. And then there were two books of poems, *When We Were Very Young* and *Now We Are Six*.

Sarah-Jane had read all these books over and over and over when she was little. Or rather—her parents had read them to her. *Winnie-the-Pooh* was too hard for little kids to read on their own. Sarah-Jane's parents had checked out the books from the library for her. But now—to have her very own copies . . .

Once she had the books, Sarah-Jane held on to them for dear life. She had been to enough tag sales to know that you couldn't put anything down. If you put something down, even for a minute, someone else could come along and snatch it up. And there wasn't anything you could do about it.

So Sarah-Jane held on tight to her books. She spotted Timothy and Titus and headed over to show them what she had found.

The odd nervousness she had felt while waiting for the doors to open was back. It was as if there was a certain tension in the air. *Why should that be when I've made up my mind what to buy?* Sarah-Jane wondered. And her nervousness was worse now—because suddenly Sarah-Jane had the shivery feeling that she was being watched.

3

Not for Sale

*F*or some reason that she couldn't quite explain, Sarah-Jane didn't go right over to her cousins. Instead, she wanted to pay for her books first. She wanted to be sure the precious Pooh books were truly hers.

So she headed toward the cashbox table to pay.

She didn't get very far.

A lady she didn't know came up to her with a friendly smile. Except to Sarah-Jane it looked kind of phony-friendly.

"Aren't those books a little young for you?" the lady asked.

Sarah-Jane just stared at her. It seemed like a pretty insulting question, and she didn't know how to answer.

"What I mean is," the lady went on quickly, "I've been looking for Pooh books for my little niece. So I would like to buy the set you have there."

Sarah-Jane hugged the books closer to her. Something was not right here. You could buy *Winnie-the-Pooh* new in any bookstore. Why did this woman want an old set? The very set Sarah-Jane had?

"I'm sorry," said Sarah-Jane. "But these books are not for sale. I need them for my old-book collection."

Until that moment, Sarah Jane hadn't even known she *had* an old-book collection. But she figured four nice old copies of *Winnie-the-Pooh* was a good way to start.

"Really!" snapped the woman. "A big girl like you should be reading books for older children and leave *Winnie-the-Pooh* for the young ones."

Sarah-Jane didn't hang around to argue with her about how easy or hard *Winnie-the-Pooh* was to read.

Instead, she pushed past the woman and practically ran all the way to the front table to pay for the books.

Just to be on the safe side, she asked for a bag and a receipt. When it came to shopping, Sarah-Jane knew what she was doing.

And she knew a bargain when she saw one.

She hurried off to show Timothy and Titus her new—old—treasures.

"You *bought* something already?" exclaimed Titus. "I don't believe it! Aren't you the one who always wanders around for hours and hours before you buy anything?"

"Yes," said Sarah-Jane. "But this time I knew exactly what I was looking for."

She opened the bag and took out the lovely little books to show them.

"*Winnie-the-Pooh!*" cried Timothy. "I remember good old Winnie. But . . . aren't these books a little young for you?"

Sarah-Jane sighed and rolled her eyes. "They're for my *collection*!"

"What collection?" asked Titus.

"My old-book collection!" said Sarah-Jane, sounding as if she couldn't *believe* he had forgotten about that.

"Oh," said Titus with a puzzled shake of his head. "I must really be losing it. I didn't even remember that you had an old-book collection."

"Well," admitted Sarah-Jane, "I haven't had it very long. . . ."

"How long?" asked Timothy.

"Uh . . . well, about ten minutes," Sarah-Jane replied.

But before she could say anything else, a man she didn't know came up to them.

Both he and the lady seemed vaguely familiar. Sarah-Jane was thinking they might have been standing behind her in the line to get in.

19

"Little girl," the man began.

Sarah-Jane frowned. She did not like the sound of this.

First one person was calling her a "big girl." And now another person was calling her a "little girl."

What was going on here?

"Uh . . . little girl—that is, I mean, young lady—I couldn't help but notice you have a nice set of books there," the man said. "How about if I give you double what you paid for them?"

He reached for his wallet, but Sarah-Jane was not impressed.

"I'm sorry," she said, slipping the books carefully back into the bag. "But they are not for sale."

After a tense moment, the man grunted, turned, and walked away. What else could he do? It was clear Sarah-Jane was not about to change her mind.

But—what in the world was going *on* here?

4

Funny Weird

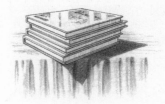

"What was *that* all about?" asked Timothy.

"I don't know," said Sarah-Jane. "It's the funniest thing. . . ."

"Funny ha-ha? Or funny weird?" asked Titus.

"Funny weird."

"What's funny weird?" asked Timothy.

"Well, that's the second grown-up this morning who's tried to get my books away from me," said Sarah-Jane. "Doesn't that seem a little weird to you?"

The boys agreed that it did.

"You know what else is a little weird, S-J?" Titus said.

"What?" asked Sarah-Jane suspiciously, sensing something was up.

"*You* are!" declared Titus.

"*ME?!*" exclaimed Sarah-Jane. What do you mean *me*?"

"I just think it's a little strange that the world's *slowest* shopper found *exactly* what she wanted the very *second* she got in the door. What gives?"

The three cousins had a detective club. To be a detective you have to be alert and observant. Which Timothy, Titus, and Sarah-Jane were—even with one another. Very, *very* little got past them.

"Yeah, S-J," said Timothy. "You said you knew exactly what you were looking for. But how did you find it so fast? It's almost as if you knew the books would be there."

"OK, OK," said Sarah-Jane. "I *did* know the books would be there. That's why I wanted to get here first thing to buy them."

"But *how* did you know?" asked Titus.

Sarah-Jane explained. "The library wanted kids to get involved in helping. So they teamed up grown-up volunteers and kid volunteers. And the pairs went door to door, collecting books. The Pooh books were some of the ones my partner and I collected. And I made up my mind right then and there that those were the ones I wanted to buy."

Sarah-Jane paused, remembering something. "Actually, come to think of it, there was something a little weird about . . ."

But she didn't have time to finish that thought.

The man and the woman who had tried to get her books were headed straight toward them.

5

First Editions

Sarah-Jane was just about to yell for help when help arrived.

Another grown-up came along.

He spoke firmly to the first two grown-ups. "All right. Why don't we all just leave this little girl alone?"

So she was back to being called a little girl. But this time Sarah-Jane didn't mind. It made her feel safe.

"Oh, sure, John!" snapped the woman. "You just want to get rid of us so you can grab the books for yourself."

"Not true," said John. "I'm not working for myself today. I'm here as a favor to the library. To make sure they don't give anything valuable away."

He looked straight at the first man, who glared back at him.

Sarah-Jane had seen lots of kid-fights at school. But it was scarier when grown-ups fought.

It seemed as if they were going to stand that way forever. But finally the man and the woman backed off.

"Probably not worth anything anyway," they muttered as they stomped right out of the multipurpose room.

Sarah-Jane heaved a sigh of relief.

"What was *that* all about?" Timothy asked for the second time that day.

"Those two!" The man shook his head. "Please believe me. We're not all like that."

"Who are you?" asked Titus.

"John Loring," said the man, handing them each a business card. "I'm a book dealer—used and rare books. In all the rush of getting the books together, Mrs. Stevens, the librarian, forgot to call me until this morning. She wanted me to look over the books and make sure they didn't sell something rare."

"So are those two. . . ?" Timothy nodded toward the door.

"They're dealers, too, I'm sorry to say," said John. "Most dealers are honest, but some aren't. They would probably have offered Sarah-Jane a few dollars for her books, knowing there was a chance they were worth a great deal more."

"The man said he would give me double what I paid for them," said Sarah-Jane. "So that would have been eight dollars. There are four books, and I paid a dollar each for them."

"May I see them?" asked John. "I promise not to run away with them."

Sarah-Jane knew that he wouldn't. So she opened the bag and pulled out the books.

John examined the books carefully. When at long last he looked up, his eyes were glittering with excitement.

"It's just as I thought!" he said. "When I saw you walking around with those books, Sarah-Jane, I wondered if they might be first editions. And I was right! First edition *Winnie-the-Pooh* in absolutely top-notch condition!"

John looked as if he might pass out from sheer excitement.

"What does 'first edition' mean?" asked Titus. "What's everybody so worked up about?"

John laughed. "We book people can get a little carried away sometimes! I admit it. But this is *truly* a find! 'First edition' means that these books belong to the first Pooh books ever printed. The books have been printed over and over again, of course, since they first came out in the mid–1920s. But these belong to the first 'batch.' They're very rare."

"So you were right," said Titus.

"I was right," said John. "And those other two characters obviously thought the same thing. But if they had gotten their hands on them, that would have been the end of it. Thank goodness you didn't sell!"

"I have no intention of selling," said Sarah-Jane crisply.

"Uh . . . well," said John. "I'm afraid it's a little more complicated than that."

6

Complications

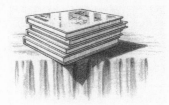

Sarah-Jane narrowed her eyes and looked hard at John.

"*What's* complicated about it?" she asked. "I bought the books with my own money."

"That's true," said John. "But the books are worth a *lot* of money."

"How much money are we talking about?" asked Titus.

John took a deep breath before he answered. "Well, I heard of a set like this that recently sold for around $13,000."

Timothy and Titus clutched their chests and staggered against the tables.

Sarah-Jane was so astonished that she almost dropped the bag.

"*What* did you say?" she gasped.

"I said $13,000," replied John with a smile.

"That's what I thought you said," gulped Sarah-Jane. "Are all old books worth that much?"

"Oh, goodness no!" said John. "Most old books aren't worth as much as new ones. It all depends on how rare the book is and how many people want it. It depends on what kind of condition it's in. It's fun to collect old books. But it's rare to find ones so . . . well, *rare*."

Timothy asked, "Is that why the dealers were here early? To see if they could snatch up any bargains?"

"That's it exactly," said John. "And there's nothing wrong with shopping for bargains. But this is a special case. Someone donated a small fortune. When Mrs. Stevens asked me to look over the books, I didn't really expect to find anything. I *certainly* didn't expect to find *these*! Or, I should say, Sarah-Jane found them."

"And I bought them with my own money," Sarah-Jane declared stubbornly.

"S-J!" cried Timothy and Titus together.

"What?" replied Sarah-Jane as if she didn't know.

"You paid four dollars for the books," said

Titus. "The books are worth $13,000. Does that sound right to you?"

"You do the math," said Timothy.

"Oh, all right, all right," grumbled Sarah-Jane. "I guess I sort of know who they belong to. And I guess I sort of know where he lives. I just don't know why he would give away such wonderful books in the first place."

"Why don't you tell me about it?" said John gently.

Sarah-Jane sighed. "OK. But it's kind of weird."

7

A Mysterious Situation

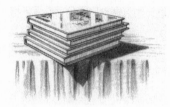

"Well, it was like this," said Sarah-Jane. "My partner, Mrs. Jackson, and I were going door to door collecting books for the book fair.

"And when we came to this house, the guy who answered the door looked *so nervous*! Mrs. Jackson said later it was as if he thought we were the 'book police' or something!

"Mrs. Jackson told him he didn't have to give us anything. But he said, no, no, that it was the duty of every law-abiding citizen to help out the public library. We thought that was a strange way of putting it. But, of course, we didn't say so.

"Anyway, we waited on the porch, and he was back in a minute with the *Winnie-the-Pooh* books. He said he was sorry he didn't have anything newer. And Mrs. Jackson said that was all right and that he didn't have to give us anything.

"But he said, no, no, he wanted to set a good example for the kids today.

"Again, we thought that was kind of a funny thing to say. But, of course, we didn't say so.

"And you want to know the *really* weird part? The guy kept calling him *Winkie*, not Winnie. Can you imagine? *Winkie-the-Pooh!*"

John looked thoughtful. "It does all sound rather strange. The books are in excellent condition—which says to me that someone has been taking very good care of them. Either that, or they've been packed away in a trunk all these years."

"They weren't packed away when we got there," Sarah-Jane pointed out. "It took him only a minute to go get them."

Timothy said, "Why would a grown-up have *Winnie-the-Pooh* sitting out?"

"He would if he were a collector of old books," said Titus. "Like Sarah-Jane here."

"It doesn't matter if I just started collecting

today," Sarah-Jane told him. "I'm still a collector. So there."

Titus just grinned at her.

"OK," said Timothy. "Let's say he's got the books sitting out because he's a collector. But if he's a collector, why give the books away? It doesn't make sense."

"How could he be a collector?" asked Sarah-Jane. "He didn't even know the name of the main character. *Winkie?* Puh-leeze! It's almost as if the books weren't his at all. He certainly didn't act like they were important to him. He actually apologized for not having anything newer to give us."

"That's odd, too," remarked John. "Book lovers usually have *lots* of books around. Surely he could have found something else to give you. The idea that someone has first-edition Pooh books—and that's *all* he has . . . Well, it just seems rather . . . weird. Sarah-Jane is right. And I must say, you kids are remarkably good at thinking things through!"

"That's because we're the T.C.D.C.," said Sarah-Jane.

"What's a 'teesy-deesy'?" asked John.

"It's letters," explained Titus. "Capital T.

Capital C. Capital D. Capital C. It stands for the Three Cousins Detective Club."

"Detectives, huh?" said John, sounding impressed. "Well, maybe the T.C.D.C. can help me figure out what to do. If this guy is the owner, we'll have to find him and give the books back. But I don't know. Something about this whole situation doesn't ring true. It just feels weird to me."

"Me, too," said Timothy.

"Me, too," said Titus.

"Me, too," said Sarah-Jane.

And that's when things got even weirder.

8

Even Weirder

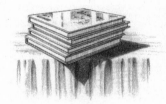

*T*he cousins and John overheard a surprising conversation.

A tall, skinny young man with light brown hair was browsing near them.

Well, *browsing* wasn't exactly the right word. It was more like *searching*.

Desperately searching.

Sarah-Jane had noticed him earlier. He had been one of the first ones in line. He hadn't picked out any books yet—even though he'd been roaming all over the room.

Just then a volunteer went up to him and asked if she could help him find something.

The young man jumped.

"Uh, no. I mean, yes. Well, maybe. I'm looking for some kids' books. See—my, um—

my sister donated them by mistake. And—um, I'd like to get them back if I can."

"Sure," said the volunteer. "What are they?"

"Um—there are four of them," said the young man. "*Winnie-the-Pooh*. I know it sounds silly, but I've had them ever since I was a kid."

Sarah-Jane gulped to keep from gasping. She glanced at Timothy and Titus. They were doing a superb job of keeping their faces blank. Not giving themselves away. This was something the detective cousins had really worked on.

"I haven't seen them," said the volunteer. "But why don't you give your name, address, and phone number to Mrs. Stevens? She's our head librarian. And she might be able to track them down for you."

"Uh—yeah, um—maybe I will—uh— later," said the young man. "I'm just going to sort of—um—look around some more."

The volunteer shrugged and turned away.

Silently Sarah-Jane tugged on John's sleeve and cocked her head. Meaning, I-have-something-to-tell-you-let's-go-over-here-where-

that-guy-can't-hear-us.

Very, very casually, John and the cousins moved out of earshot.

Even so, Sarah-Jane didn't want to talk out loud.

"That's not him!" she whispered.

"What?" said John, Timothy, and Titus together, also keeping their voices low.

"That's not him!" repeated Sarah-Jane. "That's not the guy who donated the books! The guy Mrs. Jackson and I talked to was short and kind of scruffy-looking with dark hair. And there was no sister. I don't know what this guy is talking about!"

John said, "Well, maybe if he gives his name and address to Mrs. Stevens, we can get this whole thing straightened out."

But the young man didn't go toward Mrs. Stevens' office.

Instead, he looked across the room in alarm and left in a hurry.

The cousins looked around to see what had frightened him. But all they saw was a kindly-looking old gentleman who was also intently searching through the books.

Sarah-Jane hugged the Pooh books closer, glad that they were out of sight in the bag. But she didn't feel they were safe. Not at all.

9

Whose Books?

*I*t was as if John read her mind.

"Our first order of business," he said, "is to put these books in a safe place—not that Sarah-Jane isn't taking good care of them. She is. But I feel a little nervous carrying them around."

"Mrs. Stevens has a safe in her office. We could ask her to put the books in there," suggested Sarah-Jane.

Mrs. Stevens was a good friend of Sarah-Jane's. After all, Sarah-Jane had been coming to the library week in and week out since before she could even talk. If anyone on the planet loved books more than Sarah-Jane did, it was Mrs. Stevens.

The librarian positively gasped when she

saw the books. And the way she touched them—you would have thought they were made of gold and diamonds.

"Oh! These are lovely!" she murmured. "How in the world did they end up at the book fair?"

"That's what we're trying to find out," said Sarah-Jane. "I talked to the guy who donated them. But now another guy is saying his sister donated them. The volunteer told him to give you his name, address, and phone number. But he didn't do that. He just ran out of there."

Mrs. Stevens shook her head. "That seems odd, doesn't it? If you were in that situation, it seems that you would certainly ask for help."

"Well, he was just looking around by himself," said Titus.

"And he seemed pretty nervous when the volunteer asked if she could help," added Timothy.

"The thing is," John said to Mrs. Stevens, "the books are worth a small fortune. We don't want to hand them back to just anyone until we know what's going on. So Sarah-Jane came up with the good idea of putting them in the safe until we can get to the bottom of things."

Mrs. Stevens agreed that this was a good idea.

"Is it possible there could be *two* old sets of *Winnie-the-Pooh*?" she asked. But she didn't sound as if she thought this was the case.

"I suppose anything's possible," said John. "But I can't imagine there could be two rare sets of first editions at one book fair. No, I think we're talking about the same books and two different people claiming to be the owners."

"Then who's lying?" asked Titus.

"Maybe they *both* are," said Sarah-Jane. "Maybe the books don't belong to either one of them. Maybe the books belong to someone else."

"What—? You mean they're stolen?" asked Timothy.

"Well, yes, I guess maybe I do," Sarah-Jane replied, sounding a little surprised herself at the idea.

Then suddenly another idea occurred to her.

But before she could say anything, there came a gentle tap on the door.

10

Mr. Bartholomew

Sarah-Jane was closest to the door. So she opened it to find the kindly-looking old gentleman they had seen a few minutes ago.

"I'm sorry to bother you," he began as Mrs. Stevens invited him in. "My name is Alexander Bartholomew. And I thought you might be able to help me. You see, I recently lost some very valuable old books. They were stolen, actually. And I thought they might have ended up here at your book fair. I know it's highly unlikely. But stranger things have happened."

The cousins glanced at one another. A lot of strange things had happened that day.

"May I ask the titles?" said Mrs. Stevens.

Mr. Bartholomew gave a little smile.

"Now, please don't laugh when I tell you," he said. "I may look a little old for them, but they mean the world to me. It's a collection of the stories and poems of *Winnie-the-Pooh*."

No one said anything. No one could make a sound. They all just stood there staring.

And Mr. Bartholomew went on.

"You see, I was born the year the first book came out. A dear friend of the family gave the book to me. And then in the next few years he gave me the other books as they came out. So you see, they are first editions. My mother had the foresight to keep the books in good condition for me. And I have taken care of them all my life. I do love *Winnie-the-Pooh*!"

Sarah-Jane looked with interest at the old man. He had loved the same books as a little boy—long, long ago—that she had loved as a little girl—just a few short years ago. Books that she *still* loved. If Mr. Bartholomew was not too old for *Winnie-the-Pooh*, then certainly Sarah-Jane wasn't, either!

"Me, too!" she declared. "I love *Winnie-the-Pooh*, too!"

Mr. Bartholomew smiled at her, a little sadly. "Then you will understand how upset I am to have lost my precious books. They are worth quite a bit of money. But that's not what's important to me. The important thing is their sentimental value. A lot of other things were stolen at the same time. But they can all be replaced. The books can't. And I . . . well, I just thought I would check the book fair. And ask if my books might have turned up here."

The cousins and the grown-ups all looked at one another.

A third person claiming to be the owner of the Pooh books. Certainly his story sounded believable. But what should they do?

Suddenly Sarah-Jane remembered her idea.

"I need to call my uncle Bob," she said.

Timothy and Titus stared at her in some confusion.

They knew she didn't have an uncle Bob.

11

An Important Phone Call

"*H*e's not my *real* uncle," Sarah-Jane said impatiently when she saw the looks on their faces. "He's a good friend of my father's, so I just call him uncle."

"How could your father's friend help us get to the bottom of all this?" asked John. "Does he know something about old books?"

"I have no idea," said Sarah-Jane. "But he'll probably know about the stolen books. See, he's the police chief."

"Chief Endicott?" asked Mr. Bartholomew in surprise. "He's the one I talked to about my burglary."

Sarah-Jane nodded. "Right. But I just want

to double-check something with him."

Sarah-Jane had lived in the little town of Fairfield all her life. So she knew a lot of people. She knew all the librarians, of course. She even knew the mayor—a nice lady named Jill. And she knew the chief of police.

Mrs. Stevens handed her the phone.

This wasn't exactly an emergency, Sarah-Jane decided. So she didn't dial 9-1-1. Fortunately, Mrs. Stevens had the regular police number taped to the phone along with other important numbers.

When Sarah-Jane told the officer at the front desk who she was, she got put through right away.

Timothy and Titus could pretty much follow what Uncle Bob was saying just by listening to Sarah-Jane's end of the conversation.

"Hi, Uncle Bob. It's Sarah-Jane. . . . No, I'm OK. . . . My mom and dad are OK, too. . . . No, everything's fine. Except, I'm just calling because I need to ask you something. . . . OK, see, we have some stuff here that we think might be stolen. . . . At the library, the book fair. . . . With my cousins Timothy Dawson and Titus McKay. . . . I'm calling from Mrs. Stevens' office. And John Loring is here, too. . . . He's a book dealer, helping the library. . . . Right. Well, anyway, it's about these rare first editions. . . . Yes! Yes! *Winnie-the-Pooh!* . . . And the man who reported them stolen? . . . Yes, yes! That's him! Mr. Bartholomew. He's here, too. . . . But see, the reason I called is that two other guys were claiming to be the owner. . . . Short, dark hair, kind of scruffy-looking. He's the one who donated the books to Mrs. Jackson and me. . . . No, I don't know his name. I just know where he lives. . . . That little brown house on Jones Street near the park. . . . Tall, skinny, light brown hair. He was here, looking for the books. He said his sister donated them by mistake. . . . No, he ran out when he saw Mr. Bartholomew. . . . No, he wouldn't give his name or address. . . . In the safe. . . . OK. . . . Thanks, Uncle Bob."

She handed the phone to Mrs. Stevens. "Uncle Bob wants to talk to you," she said.

Then Mrs. Stevens handed the phone to a stunned Mr. Bartholomew.

Then Mr. Bartholomew handed the phone to John Loring.

When at last John hung up, he said, "Well, Mr. Bartholomew, I believe we have some books here that belong to you."

"EX-cellent!" declared Titus.

"Neat-O!" agreed Timothy.

"So cool," murmured Sarah-Jane. She was sad to see the books go. But she knew they couldn't be going to a nicer person.

Mrs. Stevens opened the safe, and John Loring took out the bag.

"How can I ever thank you?" exclaimed Mr. Bartholomew.

"Don't thank us," said John and Mrs. Stevens together. "Thank Sarah-Jane."

12

Crooks

*J*ohn Loring handed the books to Sarah-Jane so that she could hand them to Mr. Bartholomew.

Mr. Bartholomew almost cried when he saw the books.

Sarah-Jane was almost crying, too.

Timothy and Titus practically had to pry her fingers loose.

John said, "If it hadn't been for Sarah-Jane's sharp eyes, the books would have been long gone. Either some sneaky dealers would have gotten them, or the crooks would have taken them back. I think we can assume those two guys are crooks."

"I think so," said Mr. Bartholomew. "The descriptions Sarah-Jane gave Chief Endicott match the descriptions my neighbor gave of some suspicious-looking strangers in the neighborhood."

"You said you had some other things stolen?" Mrs. Stevens asked.

"Yes," said Mr. Bartholomew. "A TV. A stereo. A computer."

Titus said, "That's the kind of stuff thieves usually take. Isn't it pretty unusual for thieves to steal old books?"

"Yes," said John. "Most thieves would have no idea that old books could be valuable."

"It sounds as if those guys knew what they were doing," said Mr. Bartholomew. "But then. . . ?"

"But then—why give them away?" Timothy finished his thought.

"And then why try to get them back?" asked Titus.

"I have an idea about that," said Sarah-Jane.

Everyone turned to her, waiting for what she would say. She was, after all, the star of the moment.

"Well," said Sarah-Jane, "it has to do with the way people lie. See—usually when people lie, they tell little bits of the truth. The tall, skinny guy lied when he said his *sister* donated the books by mistake. But maybe he was telling the truth about *somebody* donating the books by mistake. Somebody who didn't know how much they were worth."

"I think I see what you're getting at, Sarah-Jane," said John. "You're saying that *one* of the thieves knew the books were worth a lot. That was the tall, skinny one, who was so desperate to get them back. But the *other* thief, the short, dark-haired one, didn't know why they had bothered to take the books in the first place."

"Exactly!" said Sarah-Jane. "He was just so nervous when Mrs. Jackson and I came to the door—probably about the burglary!—that he wanted to look like Mr. Good Citizen. And he gave us the books."

Titus said slowly, "So . . . maybe the guy who knew what they were worth was planning on selling them. And not cutting his partner in on the money."

"That would be my guess," said John.

"A dirty double-crosser," said Timothy happily. Then he added, "I always wanted to say that."

"Well, I got the feeling Uncle Bob has a pretty good idea who they are," said Sarah-Jane. "I hope he catches them. And I hope he gets the rest of your stuff back, Mr. Bartholomew."

"So do I!" the old man replied. "But I have my books back. Thanks to you! And that's what's most important."

"Books!" said John as if he had just thought of something. "I never finished looking over them. I'd better get out there!"

13

Shopping

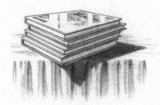

"*I*'d enjoy tagging along to see how you work, if that's all right," Mr. Bartholomew said to John.

"I'd be delighted," John replied.

The cousins thought this sounded like a plan for them, too.

Mrs. Stevens gave Sarah-Jane the money back that she had spent on the Pooh books.

All four dollars of it.

That would get her eight paperbacks.

It didn't sound so great after she had held the lovely Pooh books in her hands and planned where she would put them at home.

Still, Sarah-Jane was glad she had helped Mr. Bartholomew get his books back.

And eight paperbacks that she hadn't read

yet was a pretty good deal.

Now that all the excitement was over, she could get down to some serious shopping.

She was right about the serious shopping.

She was wrong about all the excitement being over.

14

Hunting

*J*ohn and the cousins and Mr. Bartholomew and Mrs. Stevens went back into the multi-purpose room to look through the books.

It was exciting for a little bit—thinking that they might find something valuable. But then it got pretty boring when they didn't.

John explained that this was just the way it was in the book business. You would get a little bit of success, and you would get so excited that you had to keep on looking.

"But finding first editions of *Winnie-the-Pooh*!" John exclaimed with a laugh. "That just doesn't happen!"

But, of course, it *had* happened. It had happened to Sarah-Jane.

She looked over and saw that someone had

brought in a new box of books that a busy volunteer had just emptied and set on a table.

So Sarah-Jane went over to take a look. They were kind of a hodgepodge. Mostly grown-up stuff.

And then Sarah-Jane saw something WONDERFUL.

It was an old green book—very, *very* old, by the looks of it—with gold designs on the cover. It was in excellent condition.

And best of all, it was a book of fairy tales. Sarah-Jane loved fairy tales.

She snatched up the book and hurried back to the others.

"John!" she said happily. "Look what *I* found! Isn't it pretty?"

For the second time that day, John looked as if he might pass out from sheer excitement.

15

A Bargain

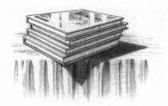

"Sarah-Jane Cooper!" John exclaimed. "I should hire you right here on the spot! You have the sharpest eyes I've ever seen. How could I have overlooked this? I'm supposed to be the book pro."

Sarah-Jane appreciated the compliment, but she didn't like the sound of this.

She said, "You didn't overlook it. The book just came in a little while ago."

"How many millions is it worth?" asked Titus.

John laughed. "If I had this book in my store, I would sell it for about $150. It's part of a set of twelve. This particular book was published in 1892."

"1892!" exclaimed Mr. Bartholomew.

"Why, that book is even older than *I* am!"

Sadly, Sarah-Jane looked down at the four dollar bills she clutched in her hand. She knew $150 was not the same as $13,000. But it was still way too much for her.

She saw her cousins looking at her.

"I know, I know," she said before Timothy and Titus could say anything. "We have to find the owner."

"Right," said Timothy. "So here we go again."

But this time finding the owner turned out to be a piece of cake.

Sarah-Jane led John back to the table where she had found the fairy tale book. But none of the other books on the table were especially valuable.

Then the volunteer pointed out the lady who had brought the books in.

John went over to her with the others following behind.

The lady looked up in surprise at this strange parade.

John handed her his card and explained about the value of the book.

Mrs. Stevens said, "You donated your

book without knowing how much it was worth. So you can certainly have it back."

"No," said the lady. "I would still like to donate it to the library. But, of course, I would like the library to get full price for it."

Again Sarah-Jane looked down at her money and at the beautiful book in John's hands. What would happen to it? Who would buy it? She sure wished she could!

"I will buy it," said Mr. Bartholomew, pulling out his checkbook. "I'll pay the library the full price for it."

That made Sarah-Jane feel a little better. At least she knew the beautiful book was going to a good home.

"And *then*," Mr. Bartholomew continued, "I will give this lovely book to my good friend Sarah-Jane. It's a thank-you for all that she has done for me today."

Everyone gasped with delight.

Timothy and Titus even clutched their chests and staggered against the tables again. (After all, how often do you get a chance to do that?)

But Sarah-Jane hesitated. Much as she wanted the beautiful book, how could she accept a present that was so expensive?

Mr. Bartholomew seemed to read her mind. "Tell you what," he said. "How about if I *sell* it to you? For—oh, say—a little less than I paid for it?"

"How much?" asked Sarah-Jane weakly. She knew she could never afford it.

Mr. Bartholomew smiled at her. There was a twinkle in his eye when he asked, "How does four dollars sound?"

"Sold!" cried Sarah-Jane, handing him the money.

She knew a bargain when she saw one.

The End